THE ANT FARM ESCAPE!

HEATHER MACHT

ILLUSTRATED BY DAVID HARRINGTON

PELICAN PUBLISHING COMPANY

GRETNA 2019

Library of Congress Cataloging-in-Publication Data

Names: Macht, Heather, author. | Harrington, David, 1964- illustrator.
Title: The ant farm escape! / by Heather Macht ; illustrated by David Harrington.
Description: Gretna : Pelican Publishing Company, 2019. | Summary: After working together to dig tunnels and build a nest, a colony of worker ants discovers they are in a child's ant farm, and must team up again to escape. Short verses are interspersed with facts about ants. | Includes bibliographical references.
Identifiers: LCCN 2018016552 | ISBN 9781455624294 (hardcover : alk. paper) | ISBN 9781455624300 (ebook)
Subjects: | CYAC: Ants—Fiction. | Ants as pets—Fiction. | Cooperativeness—Fiction.
Classification: LCC PZ8.3.M13155 Ant 2019 | DDC [E]—dc23 LC record available at https://lccn.loc.gov/2018016552

Printed in Malaysia
Published by Pelican Publishing Company, Inc.
1000 Burmaster Street, Gretna, Louisiana 70053
www.pelicanpub.com

To Raven H. and Briahna S. Macht, two tough girls building the future!—H. M.

High up near the windowsill,
a little case begins to fill,
with tiny grains of soft-beige sand
and worker ants with tools in hand!

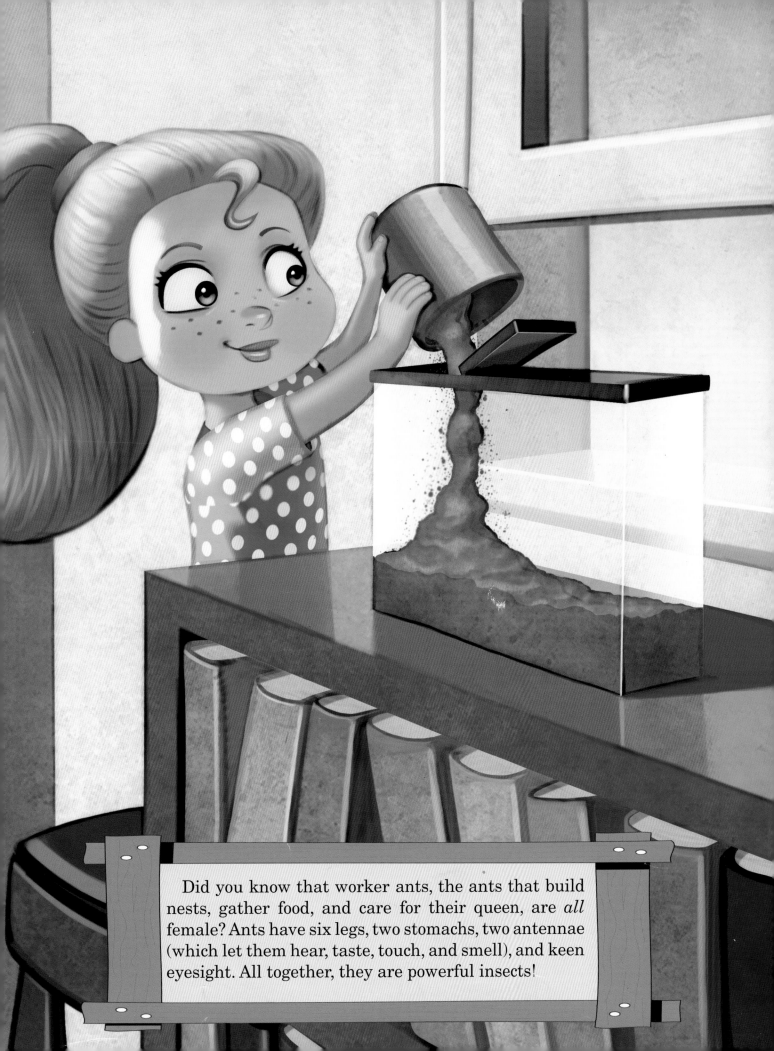

Did you know that worker ants, the ants that build nests, gather food, and care for their queen, are *all* female? Ants have six legs, two stomachs, two antennae (which let them hear, taste, touch, and smell), and keen eyesight. All together, they are powerful insects!

"Come on, all—no time to waste,"
their foreman calls; "let's move with haste!
We've got important jobs to do.
Let's break this dirt and tunnel through!"

One of the main features of ant colonies, and what makes them so successful, is their excellent use of *teamwork*. Like the foreman in this book, one leader usually guides the group of ants in the right direction.

Then, with a *heave!* and with a *ho!*
the worker ants begin to go!

Worker One lifts a pick
and strikes the ground with a *tick, tick, tick.*

The leader is not the only important part of an ant colony. Without ants that are willing to follow direction and cooperate, like the worker ants in this story, the colony would collapse.

Worker Two and Worker Three
push the dirt away quickly!

Worker Four and Worker Five
grab their shovels—time to dive.

Did you know that ants are super strong? Some species of ants can lift up to fifty times their body weight. Imagine what a group of ants working together can accomplish!

They jump headfirst, one left, one right,
and dig with all their strength and might.
Workers Six, Seven, and Eight
form a line—no time to wait!

In the wild, ants make their homes in
many different places, such as in fallen trees
and even under sidewalks.

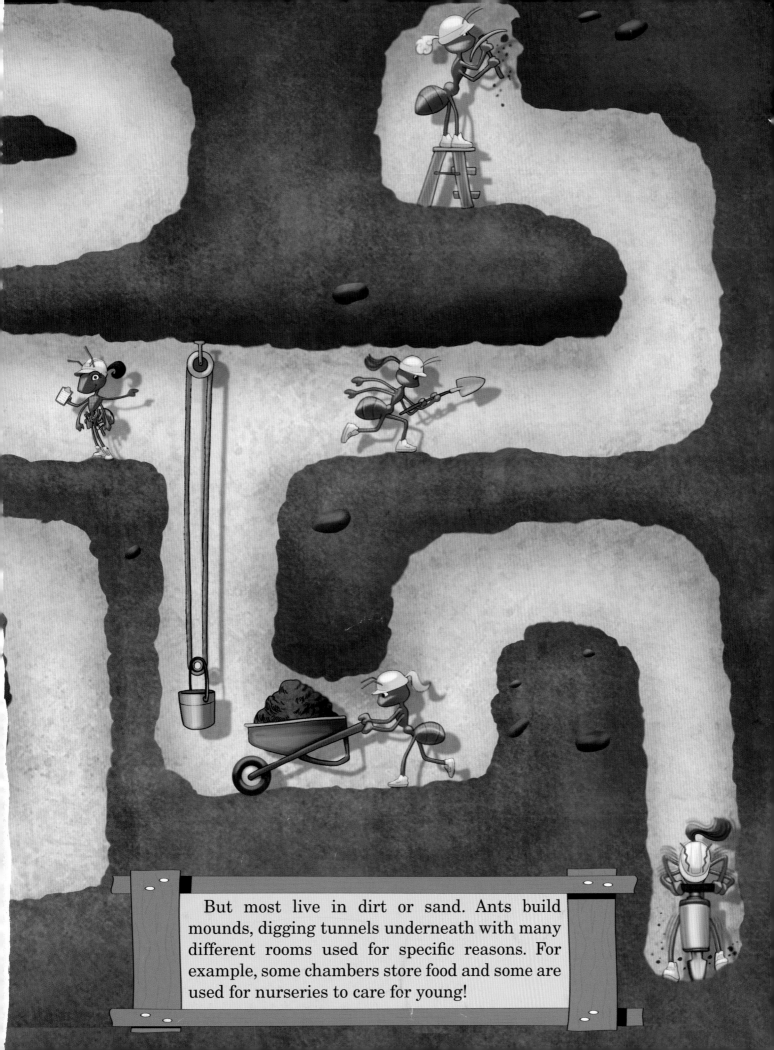

But most live in dirt or sand. Ants build mounds, digging tunnels underneath with many different rooms used for specific reasons. For example, some chambers store food and some are used for nurseries to care for young!

Grain by grain, they clear debris.
"Let's move it, gang! Come on, hurry!"

Two tunnels form, then three, then four.
"That's perfect, team. Now time to store!"

Ants eat just about anything. Most are *omnivorous*, feeding on plants, seeds, and other insects they catch. But some ants are strictly *carnivorous*, eating only prey that they hunt (such as other insects), and some are strictly *herbivorous*, eating only plants.

Beep, beep, beep! It's Worker Nine.
She's hauling food for when they dine.
Then Worker Ten rivets on their nest
a Home Sweet Home sign . . . time to rest!

While queen ants get plenty of rest, sleeping up to nine hours a day, worker ants survive on short power naps. They can nap hundreds of times a day!

But wait. What's this?! Relaxing near the windowsill,
they peek outside and see . . . *a hill?*

They look around. Their eyes grow wide.
"How can this be? We're stuck inside?!"

"All right, crew, though we've had fun,
our home belongs under the sun."
So, one by one they form a pile,
then lift the lid and flee in style!

The ants in ant farms are *only* worker ants. But ant piles in the wild contain a queen ant, female worker ants, and male drone ants, all of which are needed for the colony to survive!

There are more than *10,000,000,000,000,000* (or ten quadrillion) ants alive in the world.

Most ants are found in the great outdoors.

Now that the ants are finally free,
they'll build the home that was meant to be!
With sunlight, food, and a queen nearby,
they claim that hill. So long, goodbye!

Ants are tough insects that have survived on Earth for over 100 million years. In fact, they are considered one of the most successful creatures on the planet. They also help our environment in many ways, such as by pollinating flowers, enriching the soil, and helping to keep our gardens pest free. Here's to 100 million more years for our friends, the ants!

Bibliography

AntARK. "Ant Eating and Feeding Habits." http://antark.net/ant-life/ant-feeding.

ANTswers. "What Is an Ant Farm?" http://www.antswers.com/tag/ant-farm.

BBC Earth News. "The Secrets of Ant Sleep Revealed." http://news.bbc.co.uk/earth/hi/earth_news/newsid_8100000/8100876.stm.

Constituency of Tabaquite, The. "The Story of the Ants and Teamwork." http://tabaquiteconstituency.com/the-story-of-the-ants-and-teamwork.

"How Important Are Ants in the Environment?" http://www.heartspm.com/fascination-with/ants/ants-in-the-environment.php.

KidsKonnect. "Ant Facts." https://kidskonnect.com/animals/ant.

Stewart, Melissa. *National Geographic Readers: Ants.* Washington, D.C.: National Geographic Society, 2010.

Author's Note

When I was your age, my favorite books were the *Just Ask Book* series. I'd spend hours reading through them, admiring their pictures, and learning about our world. These books ignited my love for reading and knowledge and inspired me to become an author. I hope you enjoyed learning about ants and their role in our environment. I especially hope the young girls reading along are inspired to take an active role in building our future. May you reach for the stars as an astronaut, save the world as a scientist, be a shining example as a president, or move readers as an author. No matter your path, may you always seek to be a leader.

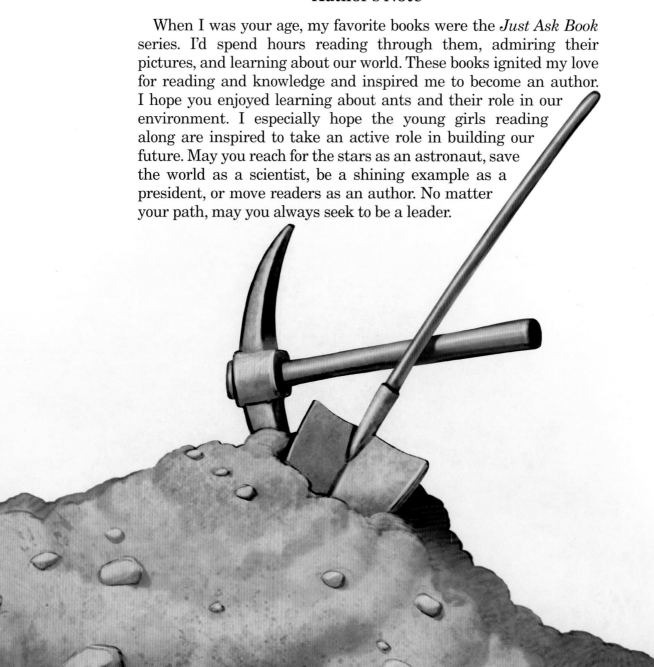